FIND YOUR WAY HOME

Fiona M Campbell

CONTENTS

Title Page 1

. . . . 5

Me and them 6

New Shoes 7

Edith 8

Memories of the promenade 13

Our Granite Guardian 14

Finn 15

Bletherin on the bus 20

Guy with the guitar 21

Hamish 22

Skye 28

Bennachie 32

Acknowledgement 35

Stay at home, they said
But what if you don't have one?
Where do you keep safe?

Me And Them

Just me
Lying in doorway of abandoned shop
And them
Rushing past, late for work

Just me
Second-hand clothes, worn shoes
And them
Smart suit, designer trainers

Just me
Empty tummy, dry lips
And them
Costa coffees, Subway sandwiches

Just me
No-one to care, no-one to call
And them
iPhone attached to ear

Just me
Lost, lonely, pointless
And them
Following dreams, living lives

Spare a smile
A kind word, a cup of tea
One day
I might be you, you might be me

New Shoes

Barefoot, blistered and bleeding
She wanders in from the street
People stare, flabbergasted
Very odd, unheard of in fact

She doesn't know her size
So like Cinderella, she tries them on
Randomly selecting pretty colours

Silvery, glittery heels
She twirls for the mirror
Sales assistant sighs

Wellingtons for the garden
If she had one
Satin ice skates
She would glide on the icy pond
Pretty sandals
To feel the sand between her toes

Boring, black brogues
Perfect!

With no pennies in her pocket
She wanders back to the street
Barefoot, blistered and bleeding

Edith

Edith's fingers were numb and white, and she could see her breath in the night air. Whatever had she been thinking? She could have been sitting at home reading Women's Weekly with the heating on but couldn't face her empty house. She'd taken only the contents of the emergency biscuit tin and her purse, leaving her bank cards behind. These things were far too easy to trace, and Edith didn't want to be found.

The number forty-four bus had taken her to the city centre, then she'd caught one of those mega buses all the way from Edinburgh to Aberdeen. It was such a pretty city with all the granite buildings and so near to the seaside. The bus stopped right outside St. Nicholas Church, the perfect place for her first night. Edith took her time reading the gravestones. Some had been taken so young, but even the old had left loved ones behind. She had been looking for God to guide her and keep her safe, but instead there was an aura of death. She couldn't sleep there surrounded by it.

A short walk around the corner and down some stairs took her underneath Union bridge. It was a hub for equally troubled souls. She wondered about their stories. What had brought them here? Folding her blanket into a makeshift pillow, she placed her shoes neatly together by her side, snuggled into her coat and drifted off to sleep. When she woke, her shoes and bag had vanished.

Realising she needed a plan, Edith found herself a step, nestled between the book shop and the bank. The West end was a hub of lawyers and estate agents with mobile phones permanently attached to their ears. They seldom carried small change now they had credit and debit cards, but Edith smiled when she realised her blanket held enough coins to buy a hot drink. The café blackboard promised an endless list of beverages; espressos, lattes, and cappuccinos, but nothing could beat a nice, strong cup of tea. To take away, of course, they made it clear she wasn't welcome to sit inside.

Feeling outcast and unwanted was unfamiliar to a woman who had been surrounded by love and kindness. After a good half hour of weeping, she decided not to resign herself to a sad and lonely existence, watching other people live their lives and hoping they would take pity on her. Instead, Edith promised herself that every day would hold a new adventure. The perfect ladies at the perfume counter stared aghast, as she indulged in a spritz of their newest scent. As a little treat, she made a few extra trips up and down the escalator, before gazing in awe at the vast array of clothes before her. A whole new world of pretty colours and material. She wandered around exploring everything, selecting a pretty polka-dot skirt and a turquoise, silk blouse and holding them up, so she could see herself in the mirror. She heard the young sales assistants whispering and struggling to contain their giggles. Her dearest wish was to look like herself again, but new clothes weren't the answer. After a few months on the street, rotten teeth, matted hair, and a repugnant stench had become part of her essence.

Edith found some secrets which always brightened her day. Hidden behind the supermarket, a row of coloured bins became her treasure trove. She filled her bag with sandwiches; tuna and mayonnaise, chicken and sweetcorn, cheese and pickle. What a find! The blue bin harboured unsold newspapers. She added one to her collection. Reading wasn't her forte, but she visited the library every week, enjoying the warmth and silence, as she looked at the pictures. Her mouth watered as she browsed through cookbooks filled with delicious food. For a moment, she could escape and visit anywhere in the world. Her imagination took her to sunny beaches and special sights, visiting the Leaning Tower of Pisa, the Empire State Building, and the Eiffel Tower. Harry had promised they would go on a cruise when they retired, but when the time came, they had little savings and were both content with a cottage in York.

In the evening, when the church bells chimed seven, Edith made her way to His Majesty's theatre. She watched young lovers and elderly companions with hands entwined and families filled with excitement. As she crept down the stone staircase to the stage door, the walls were covered with graffiti and the ground was littered with cigarette butts and discarded needles. Nevertheless, the music from the performance could be heard perfectly. Anything from Mozart to musicals and not a penny to pay. Harry used to play Mozart for her. She closed her eyes and remembered.

Directly opposite Edith's step was the charity shop and she enjoyed watching the elegant older lady dress the window. She often gave her a wave, but Edith had never felt brave enough to go inside. Until one blustery autumn day, when the window was decorated with red and gold. All day, Edith gazed at the red heels beneath the mannequin. They reminded her of Dorothy in 'The Wizard of Oz'. If only it was easy as clicking your heels and finding yourself at home. The rain began as gentle droplets, but only moments later it was relentless. The business folk donned their smart, black umbrellas. Edith packed her belongings into her black bag and headed towards the window of the charity shop. The small canopy above offered a little shelter, but she longed to go inside. What harm would it do? She had no money to offer, but she could enjoy the warmth as she looked around. Edith put her hand to her lips. There were so many shoes. Rows and rows of different styles. Her stomach danced with a fluttering sensation that she had not experienced for a long time.

'Feel free to try them on,' Helen offered.
Edith pointed to the red heels in the window.
'I don't think they're your size, dear. How about these?'
Edith laid her bag beside her and sat on the chair. She used her skirt to rub the worst of the dirt off her swollen, painful feet, before sliding them into the stretchy slippers. They reminded her of ballet pumps.

'Edith James, step forward please,' said Mrs McConnachie.
Ten little girls stood in a row, with their hair in tight buns and dressed in black leotards and pink tutu skirts. Her new ballet shoes were the perfect present for her eighth birthday. Just like a real ballerina, she could point her toes perfectly.
'Three demi pliés and one sauté please, Edith'
'Bravo, bravo, my prima ballerina.'

Her knee cracked, as she bent down to remove the slippers. What next? Which should she choose? Helen smiled in amazement. Suddenly, the old woman was as sprightly as a teenager. Trying on the pink, summer sandals took her back to building sandcastles and splashing in the waves. They were staying in a caravan, mum, dad and her little brother, Joe. There was so much to explore. Walking hand in hand with her brother, they took their nets to the rock pools and filled their buckets with crabs and shells.

It was impossible to resist the lure of white lace bridal shoes with silver diamante. Edith felt like an ugly sister trying Cinderella's slipper, but she persevered. The wedding march resounded in her head. Her father proudly walking her down the aisle in the quaint, village church.

'Edith James, do you take Harry Wilson to be your wedded husband to live together in marriage? Do you promise to love him, comfort him, honour and keep him for better or worse, for richer or poorer, in sickness and health and forsaking all others, be faithful only to him so long as you both shall live?'

She had meant every word. Harry was her forever love and they had enjoyed a happy marriage. She was his darling Edie and Harry was her honey. They were blessed with children, one of each. Frankie loved fishing with his Daddy and Flora loved to bake with her Mummy. Their family would sit in church every Sunday, the envy of many. They had their fair share of troubles. Losing their parents, Harry losing his job and Frankie getting sick. Somehow, Edith always managed to find a silver lining. Later years took them to a lovely bungalow with a garden to be proud of. They would work together pruning roses and planting pansies with a flask of tea. The children moved on and had families of their own. They had three precious grand babies to spoil.

Harry was always the smart one. He kept abreast of the local news and completed the crossword religiously. He was the one who paid the bills and organised everything and that was the way Edith liked it. Until gradually, he couldn't find the right words and final reminders arrived in the mail. He couldn't find his glasses, when they were right there on his face and he left the milk out without its lid. She told herself it was just old age. It would come to us all, but when he wandered off in his pyjamas and asked where his wife was, Edith realised that something was very wrong.

Alzheimer's was a cruel disease which stole her husband piece by piece. To the point where he was unrecognisable. Each night, she lay beside his familiar body, but he pushed her away.

'Don't touch me. I don't know you.'

She became little more than a nurse. Dressing him, brushing his teeth, and cutting up his food. It was a thankless and monotonous life. The GP sent a social worker to check how they were getting on. Then they took her Harry away.

'It's for the best, Mum, you'll see.' Best for who? Her daughter, Flora, meant well, but Edith and Harry had been muddling along quite nicely. Who gave those interfering busybodies the right to make choices for them? She'd only needed to look into his kind brown eyes and feel his strong hand squeezing hers to know that her Harry was still in there.

Admittedly, it hadn't always been easy, but they had adapted and made things work. Too many steak and kidney pies and fish suppers had taken their toll on Harry, so getting him upstairs had no longer been an option. That was why they'd taken to sleeping downstairs. Harry sprawled on the big sofa and Edith on the armchair. She hadn't worried about his little accidents. They had plenty of clean sheets.

   Not safe, they'd said. A danger to himself. It wasn't as though he had planned to abseil from the bedroom window. There was that time when he relieved himself on Mrs Harold's roses, but he hadn't been allowed outside after that. Edith was almost certain that Peggy Harold was the culprit. Ever since her Jimmy went off with that young barmaid, she'd been more concerned with everyone else's business than her own. The lady from the social wouldn't give any names, but who else could it have been?

   They'd come for Harry with a wheelchair, but there was nothing wrong with his legs. It was his mind which had failed him. Edith had stood in the hallway and wept. She should have fought harder, maybe paid for a fancy lawyer. Harry belonged with her, where he had been for forty-five years. Who were they to say it would end like this? Harry would have been happy at home until the good Lord called him.

The eight-thirty bus delivered her daily to Meadowbank nursing home, where she got on with her knitting and chatted to Harry. She read him the newspaper and they listened to the radio. Edith couldn't understand why he couldn't do all that at home. Her vegetable broth was so much more nutritious than the watery concoction they offered, and she wasn't even allowed to bring in the fish and chips for their Friday treat.

On Thursday the twenty-fourth of April at quarter to ten, the phone rang. Harry had aspiration pneumonia, they said, which was common in Alzheimer's patients. All going well, he would be back in the home in a couple of days. Nobody told her what the worst-case scenario would be. When Edith entered the room, his eyes were closed, and he was attached to all sorts of machinery. She had taken his hand and kissed it, as she always did, but there was no response. His breathing alternating between deep and slow and rapid and quiet, as if there were two people in the bed. Kind, loving Harry, fighting to come back to her and the angry stranger who was trying to steal him. Edith prayed for a miracle which didn't come. She wasn't even there when he took his final breath.

   She wore a yellow dress to the funeral. It was Harry's favourite. Edith assured everyone that she was fine, but she was most definitely was not. The house was lonely, and she had never been alone. She'd been a young, naïve nineteen-year old when Harry proposed, and she had left her parents for their new life together. She didn't like this at all. No-one to talk to and nothing to do. Flora had insisted she move in with them, but she didn't want to be a burden. It wasn't fair to interrupt their lives. Besides, Edith had always been a free spirit.

   So early one Monday morning, she took a black bin bag from the drawer and grabbed a fleecy white blanket, which still smelled like Harry. She lifted a photo frame from the hallway table but thought better of it. That was her Harry, and he didn't exist anymore. Dressed in her favourite coat and a red head scarf, she closed the door for the last time.

'Are you alright, my dear?' Helen asked.

Tears trickled down Edith's cheeks, as she sat surrounded by the myriad of unwanted shoes.

'Here, have a tissue and I'll make us a nice cup of tea.'

Edith's voice was a whisper. It had been so long since she had spoken to anyone.

'He was my forever and always, you know.'

'How lovely. How long were you married?'

'Forty-five wonderful years'

Helen was a good listener and Edith felt comfortable chatting to her.

'Have you heard of The Hope project?' said Helen, placing her hand on Edith's. 'I've heard so many stories about people getting back on their feet with their help. I'll come with you if you like.'

The following morning, the two women walked through the welcoming doors of St. Nicholas Church. The smell of bacon butties and fresh soup was enticing, but Edith needed to do something first. She smiled, as the sun glistened through the stained glass and lit a candle, as she offered a prayer for Harry. She could say goodbye and allow herself to carry on without him by her side.

'Are you ready?' Helen asked and Edith knew she was. It was time to go home.

Memories Of The Promenade

Treasure basket in my hand
Tiny footprints in the sand
My favourite adventure

A handful of coppers for slot machines
A perfect, swirly ice-cream
My goldfish in a plastic bag

A quaint café on the street
Where teenage friends would often meet
My first true love

The lonely beach, my sanctuary
As I send my tears out to the sea
My first broken heart

Seventeen, I learn to drive
Independence at last arrives
My car, my freedom

And now full circle, I return
Time for my little ones to learn
Find treasures and make memories.

Our Granite Guardian

Majestically, he sits

A perfect entrance to the street where culture abounds

Men in suits accompany ladies in splendid dresses

As they enter a world of red and gold

Talented thespians transport them to an alternate reality

Leaving their predictable lives behind

On the other side, eclectic art lovers

Peruse random interpretations of life

Musing the hidden meaning behind the endless strokes

And for those with a thirst for knowledge

Whether scholar or internet explorer

Hundreds of bookshelves await

Fantasy, history, drama, and poetry

Around the corner, Robert Burns

Our Scottish baird in bronze resides

And William Wallace, a true patriot

Stands ceremoniously above the entrance

To the beautiful gardens below

The granite lion war memorial outside the Cowdray Hall, Aberdeewas designed by sculptor, William Macmillan RA (1877-1927)

Finn

Elise smiled as a couple approached her desk, their hands entwined, faces emanating a glow, following their romantic and relaxing weekend.

'Thank you for a truly wonderful stay,' he said, handing over their room key.

'I'm glad you've enjoyed it,' she said. 'We hope to see you again soon.'

Her new boss patted her on the back. 'That's the spirit, dear. How have you enjoyed you first day with us?'

'It's been lovely, thank you. Everyone's made me feel so welcome and there's such a magical ambience in the hotel.'

'Glad to hear it,' he said. 'Now, call it a day and we'll see you tomorrow.'

Elise went to the bathroom to freshen up before heading home. She ran her brush through her long, black hair and painted her lips with burgundy lipstick. When she'd applied for this job, she hadn't imagined they would choose her, a quiet Scottish girl, to be the front-of-house manager at one of the most prestigious hotels in Oxford. She was no stranger to the successful running of a hotel, having spent much of her teenage years helping her parents at their family lodge in the Highlands. It had been assumed that she would continue working there when she finished school, but Elise had dreams of her own to follow. Her heart took her to London to follow her dream of singing in a West End show. Three years at stage school had been amazing, but after copious auditions, she was still waiting for her big break. Her parents had convinced her to follow a different path in the meantime. As she collected her coat from the staff room, she paused for a moment to admire the breath-taking view from the window. The cultural buildings were worlds away from the lochs and hills of home. Footsteps behind her interrupted her daydream.

'Sorry, I hope I didn't startle you,' said the handsome man, offering his hand. 'I'm Riley, I manage the restaurant.'

'Nice to meet you,' she said, tingles rippling through her, as they shook hands. There was no wedding ring, she noted, wondering if he would feature in the new chapter of her life.

Having wished good night to the evening staff, they walked out to the street, alongside the stunning Georgian façade of the hotel. Noticing a man curled under a blanket, Elise fumbled in her bag for her purse,

'I wouldn't bother,' said Riley. 'We don't want him to make a habit of sitting there. Besides, you know your money will only provide his next beer.'

Dismissing him, Elise placed a five-pound note in the upturned hat on the pavement. Behind the untamed facial hair, were kind, green eyes. What was his story? she mused.

'Can I give you a lift somewhere?' Riley offered, pointing his keys towards the red convertible opposite them.

'No thanks,' she said. His shallow manner evidently didn't match his good looks.

When she arrived at work the next morning, he was there, nestled between two plant pots. A plethora of people passed without a glance in his direction. Boasting designer labels and apple I-phones, yet seemingly not having a copper to spare. Elise wanted to help but couldn't afford to hand out money every morning. Instead, she handed over her home-made cheese and pickle sandwich. He smiled. One of those real smiles, which made his green eyes sparkle and warmed her heart. And so, it began. Each morning she would prepare two lunches: sandwiches, fruit and the occasional packet of crisps.

February was proving to be very cold. Much to the delight of her flatmate, Mina, Elise spent Sunday afternoon making a pot of her mother's famous Scotch Broth. It smelled delicious and made her homesick for the lilting Scottish accents and the family she'd left behind. On Monday morning, she donned her new knee length leather boots and her umbrella. She was surprised to see him there, in his usual spot, despite the weather.

'Morning,' she said, handing over a silver travel mug filled with the hot broth.

'Morning,' he said. 'Thank you, Angel.' She was surprised to hear the velvet tone, having expected a rough, husky voice to match his rugged exterior. Perhaps she was more judgemental than she thought.

'I'm no angel,' she said laughing. 'I'm Elise McCarthy.'

'Finn' he said, smiling as an elderly lady dropped a pound in his hat.

'I hope you don't think I'm being nosy but isn't there anywhere inside you can go on a day like this. You'll get ill sitting around in wet clothes.'

'I need to make ten pounds for a night in the shelter,' he explained.

'Oh. I'm sorry,' she said, doubting that was even a possibility, given the lack of generosity around here.

'Why are you apologising? It's not your fault,' he said.

'I need to go,' she said, noticing that Riley was beckoning her from across the street.

'Morning, 'he said, 'I was wondering if I could sneak under your umbrella.'

Riley had dropped copious hints about going for a drink and joining him at his gym, but she'd managed to avoid them so far, feigning other plans and illness. Elise was beginning to wish she had conjured up an imaginary boyfriend. Valentine's day was looming, and every shop window boasted hearts and roses. Having been brought up with fairy tales and Disney princesses, only a handsome prince would suffice. However, reality was teaching her to lower her expectations. When the fourteenth arrived, she was looking forward to a movie night and Chinese take-away with Mina. A celebration of being single. The hotel lobby was filled with more magic than usual. Every room was booked for the night. She welcomed couples excited by new love and elderly companions, whose love was timeless. The highlight of her day had been meeting the secret celebrities who would be enjoying the suite. She had to admit to feeling a little envious, as she watched the happy couples make their way to the restaurant for dinner in stunning dresses and elegant tuxedos.

'You shall go to the ball,' said Riley, walking towards her.

'I was planning to go home to bed,' she said, with an exaggerated yawn.

'Come on, Elise. You only live once!'

She handed over to her colleague and followed Riley through to the restaurant. She felt uneasy about eating there. It didn't feel appropriate to eat at her workplace, besides the fact that she was extremely under-dressed. He led her out to the terrace, where the view of the city was spectacular.

'Wine, Madam?' he asked, pouring her a glass of the house red.

This wasn't the evening she had imagined, but how could she refuse, when he had gone to so much effort.

'I devised the menu, you know. The boss said it was innovative and appetizing.'

They started with a delicious pork and apple terrine, accompanied by a spiced plum chutney. She had to agree that it was a mouth-watering combination.

'I bet that's one of the best things you've ever eaten,' he said, nudging her playfully, but hard enough to make her say 'ow' in her head.

The waiter brought two plates with steak in a black pepper sauce and green beans and sweet potato mash.

'Please tell me you're not a veggie freak,' said Riley.

Elise was too fond of her mother's steak pie to even contemplate that. She could swear there was a hint of cinnamon in the mash and the steak was cooked to perfection. It was easy to see why Riley had been hired, despite his egocentric personality. Even after a couple of glasses of wine, she wasn't feeling remotely attracted to him. His conversation over dinner had revolved around his car and the performance of his favourite football team and she'd had to stifle a yawn. Dessert was a delicious mango and passion fruit panna cotta. The food had surpassed her expectations. She hoped he wasn't going to charge her but wouldn't have been surprised if he did.

'So, shall we go back to mine?' he said, as they left the hotel.

'I'm going to pass if you don't mind but thank you for a lovely meal,' said Elise, turning to walk in the opposite direction.

Riley shook his head. 'Are you kidding me? You've sat in front of me all evening, tossing your hair and giving me seductive looks. You can't tease a guy like that.'

He held her against the wall. 'Wait, you're playing hard to get, aren't you?'

His forceful lips silenced Elise before she could protest. Placing her hand on his chest, she tried to push him away. 'Riley, stop I'm not interested.'

Her heart was thumping, and she struggled to catch her breath as panic set in. The busy, cultural hub was now dimly lit and deserted. Anyone passing by would mistake the scene for a passionate end to a romantic evening.

She could make out a figure walking towards them and a familiar voice. 'Elise. Is everything okay?'

She shook her head, fighting back tears.

'I think it's time you went home,' Finn said, placing his hand on Riley's shoulder.

'Get your disgusting hands off me. Why does this guy even know your name, Elise? I warned you not to give him any money. Now he thinks he owns the street. Of course, it's not like he's got anywhere else to go. Well, you can have her. I've wasted enough of my time.'

She watched Riley drive off at speed. He'd been drinking far too much to be safe at the wheel.

'You're shaking,' said Finn, offering his blanket.

'I'm okay,' she said. 'Thanks to you. Do you have somewhere to go tonight?'

'I had a date lined up, but she cancelled at the last minute,' he said, laughing.

'You know what I mean,' she said.

'It wasn't a good day today,' he said, rubbing his eyebrow. I didn't have enough for the shelter and St Mark's was full. They only have twenty spaces free.'

'Come in,' she said. 'I think we could both use a drink.'

Discreetly placing his backpack and blanket behind the front desk, Elise led him through to the bar. A few guests gave them a second glance, but they managed to find a quiet table in the corner. Elise told Jed, the bar man, what had happened and how Finn had rescued her.

'Someone should have warned you. Riley's got quite a reputation,' he said, pouring two whiskies.

Her instincts had been right. She wished she had refused to be a part of his Valentine fantasy. The whisky was warm in her chest and she began to feel calmer. Her dad swore it was the cure for anything.

'That definitely hits the spot,' said Finn, 'but I would love a cup of coffee.'

'I'm sure that can be arranged,' said Elise.

She asked the girl on the desk to arrange for coffee to be brought to them and they made their way to the guest library.

'I've always wondered what the hotel looked like on the inside,' he said. 'It really is stunning, isn't it?'

'Have a seat,' she said, pointing at the comfortable sofa. 'This is my favourite room. I love books. Classics, thrillers, romance. It's the way they can take you to another world, away from the problems of this one. I don't suppose you get much opportunity to read.'

'I used to, especially poetry. My wife owned a bookshop.' It was the first time she'd heard him talk about himself. She hadn't wanted to pry. The circumstances that led him to the street were no-one's business but his own. He said owned. Perhaps she wasn't in his life anymore, but then again, he was wearing a wedding ring.

'Sorry to interrupt,' said Anna, placing the tray with coffee and biscuits on the table. 'Enjoy the rest of your evening.'

'I used to read lots,' he continued, 'before everything…before Marie.'

He was obviously struggling. 'You don't have to share anything you're not comfortable with. I'm just so, so grateful for your help tonight.'

'Not as grateful as I am to you. It's not just the lunch. Your smile brightens my day. People stop and throw a couple of coins at me, but they don't look me in the eye, you know. They look at me like I'm a piece of litter spoiling their environment or something horrid on the bottom of their shoe. Just a thing. A nuisance. Not a person. Not someone worthy of their time. Worthy of a kind word or a smile.'

Elise felt tears pricking her eyes. Who was this man? He didn't deserve be living that life. 'It's okay, Finn. I want to help you. What can I do?'

'I actually met Marie in the library when we were both studying English at university. We had almost fifteen wonderful years together. When we opened the bookshop, I gave up lecturing to concentrate on my writing. Then Marie found the lump and it spread fast and when she was gone, there was no point in anything anymore. There was nothing left to pay the bills and the phone calls and letters were incessant, demanding money I didn't have.'

'I'm so, so sorry,' she said, wiping a tear. He had obviously been very much in love with his wife and everything had just spiralled out of control.

'It was okay. I put everything away in a box in my mind. My only focus is getting enough money for the shelter. It's for the best. If I think about her and how things should have been…'

'I understand, but you shouldn't have to live like this. Everyone deserves food and shelter and someone to care about them'

Her eyes met his and they shared a moment. A promise of a new beginning. Since the hotel was fully booked, she decided to order a taxi. Finn could spend the night at her flat. Elise knew she was taking a risk. Everything he'd just told her could be lies, but she was indebted to him for his help. Tonight, he had been her hero. Maybe now she could be his.

Elise pressed snooze as her seven 'o' clock alarm woke her. She cursed herself for leaving it set on her day off. Snuggling back under the duvet, she remembered she had a stranger sleeping on her sofa. Putting on her pink, fluffy dressing gown, she crept through to the living room. Finn was snoring loudly, and Mina was gesturing 'what on earth?' from the kitchen. 'Long story,' Elise mouthed.

After a haircut, a shower and a shave, Finn looked like a completely different man. 'It's like a cloud has lifted,' he said. 'I'm ready to give life another shot.' Elise placed a gentle kiss on his cheek, hoping that this was the beginning of her fairy-tale romance.

Bletherin On The Bus

Foo ye daien? I've nae seen ye in donkeys
Faur ye gaen the day then?
Div ye nae min that I ging for a muckle messages on a Friday?
I aye pick up ma fish fae the market an ma rowies fae the baker

Faur ye gaen on this bus onywy?
I have tae get new glaisses
I cannae see onything at a these days
How can I keek oot ma windae withoot ma glaisses?

Did ye hear aboot Jimmy Broon?
He's deid ye ken- a fine man wis Jimmy
Fit ye battin yer gums aboot?
Jimmy Broon wis in the Coopie last week!

Fit aboot thon Irish lassie fa still bides wi her ma?
Elsie telt me that she's expecting a bairn ony day noo
An her nae married! I heard it was the postie
Niver! It was thon laddie wi the holes in his lugs

You'll niver guess fa I sa at the bingo the ither nicht
Div ye min on Francis? Well she telt me that Maggie telt her that
Jessie's got a new bidie in and he's nae e'en half her age
Dearie me! Fit a palava, we're owre old for that malarkey

Foo's your Bert daien?
He's aye moanin and aye makin a mess
Fit aboot George?
Jist the same, getting on ma nerves and ne'er liftin a finger

I should've listened tae ma da and ne'er married him in the first place
Bert still kens foo tae tickle ma fancy- wi daffies fae the gairden and a strawberry tairt
That aye dis the trick!
Ken fit? Ah think I'll pick him up a pokey chips fae the Ashvale on ma way hame

Guy With The Guitar

A lost boy, a guitar his only friend
Is begging on this street where his story ends?
Strumming on the corner with calloused hands
Imagining a stage for him and his band

Can't you see that he's afflicted?
He didn't mean to become addicted
Pills promise to take away the pain
And magical needles which enter his veins

Each passing day, he craves it more
His heart empty, his body sore
What started as a want has become a need
When he stole from you, it wasn't just greed

He's looking for a way to stay alive
The only way he knows how to survive.
They look at him the way they look at trash
Not worthy of a penny of their hard-earned cash

What do you they care if he's drunk or high?
Who will even notice if he lives or dies?

Hamish

The lights twinkled in the winter wonderland window, as Hamish McLeod, a dishevelled young man, lay in fitful slumber. 'M & S' was, without doubt, the prime location for a busker on Christmas Eve. As day dawned, he rolled up his sleeping bag and removed the padlock from his guitar. Already, there was a queue of hopeful shoppers. Men who had memorised underwear sizes, those looking for a gift set for granny and the working mums, clasping their ticket for turkey and thanking God for pre-prepared veg.

Placing the rainbow strap over his head, he rubbed his lucky plectrum between his fingers. Absentmindedly, he stroked the tweed scarf around his neck. It carried fond memories of family and their life on the island. Surrendering to the music, his fingers began to strum. Even among the panic of present buying, people felt compelled to stop and listen to his lilting voice, taking a moment to store some Christmas magic. Occasionally, children would be sent to throw a penny in his hat. In this age of wallets packed with plastic, carrying notes and loose change was rare. It was never about the money for Hamish. This was just a stepping stone on the road to his big break. That day in his future, when someone would finally recognise his talent and he could prove his parents wrong. He shivered at the thought of digging peat to tend the fire and herding sheep at the croft. Singing one of his own songs was nerve wracking, but he was keen to see how the audience reacted. A heartfelt ballad about those we miss at Christmas. As he poured emotion into the words, he could see it was touching people. Some rubbed away silent tears, as they recognised the story in their own lives. The applause which followed was overwhelming. Hamish was so lost in the moment that he failed to register the two uniformed officers approaching him.

'Morning, permit please?'

Nightmare! A year singing on the street and he'd never been stopped before.

'Sorry, I don't…'

'Then I suggest you pack up, mister.'

'Hey, it's Christmas, can't you let me off, just this once?'

The crowd were becoming increasing irate, chanting 'let him sing, let him sing.'

'Just give it up, man,' He heard his friend. Dante, shout above the crowd.

From the scowl on his face, Hamish could tell that P.C Rogers was already miffed at having to work on Christmas Eve,

'Alright, that's enough, just hand over your guitar and that'll be the end of it.'

'You've got to be kidding? It's all I've got!' said Hamish, tightening his grip on his prized possession.

'Obstructing the course of justice?' the officer asked his colleague.

Just my luck, thought Hamish, as he was cuffed and escorted to the van.

A larger lady with arms full of shopping bags pushed to the front of the crowd.

'Have a heart,' she shouted at the officers. 'It's Christmas for goodness sake.'

'Just doing our job, dear. Now you get yourself home and have a lovely Christmas.'

'Listen. I've got a spare room and I'll make sure he doesn't cause you any more trouble. Take the cuffs off him. It's hardly the crime of the century is it?'

P.C. Rogers looked at his watch. Another half hour and his shift would be over.

'It's your lucky day, mate,' he said, as he removed the handcuffs. 'Don't let me see you back here without a permit though.'

'Right,' said Ruth, 'what should I call you?'

'Hamish. Hamish McLeod and thanks for…you know,' he said.

'No worries. I wouldn't let my dog be treated like that. Seeing as you've got your sleeping bag there, I'm guessing you've got nowhere to go tonight. Grab your things and you can help me with these bags,' she said with a smile, 'my car's over there in the multi-storey.'

After a refreshing shower and delicious stovies with homemade oatcakes, Ruth poured them each a small glass of whisky.

'Shall we leave some cookies out for Santa?' she said, with a giggle.

With her cheery disposition, silver curls and sparkly, red blouse, Ruth was exactly how he imagined Mrs Claus would be. She would have made a wonderful friend for Nanna Rose. Hamish focussed on the mesmerising flames of the open fire, as tears pricked his eyes.

***

The fifteen-minute walk from the school bus to the croft was Hamish's favourite time of day. Usually, it was so quiet he could hear each footstep on the gravel and the ripples of the loch. Today there was a storm brewing and he had to battle against the strong wind and heavy rain. The smell of peat in the air was enticing. In a few minutes, he could get cosy in front of the fire.
Opening the wooden door, he was welcomed by muddy paws. Nothing beats the smell of wet dog, except maybe the sweet smell of freshly made porridge.

'I'm home, Nanna.'

'Anns 'a chidsin[1], Baloch.'

Nanna Rose was perfectly fluent in English, but since Papa had passed, she'd become very stubborn. 'Baloch' was her pet name for her only grandson.

'Please, Nanna, you know my Gaelic's rubbish.'

'All right then, take those boots off you and sit down. I'll get you some breakfast.'

'It smells amazing, but it's nearly dinner time,' he laughed.

Dad was busy with the animals and fixing up the tractor and mum was working late shifts at the hospital, so Nanna Rose would watch Hamish after school, or was it the other way around? It was only little things at first, wearing her coat instead of her apron, forgetting to switch the oven on, constantly asking when Papa would be home. Hamish tried to tell his parents, but they reassured him. She was bound to be showing some signs of old age at eighty-two.

It was a Thursday when he arrived home and she wasn't there. Everyone was frantic with worry. The rain was relentless, and that wind could knock you of your feet. It promised to be a really cold night and Rose could be too frail to survive it. Word spread quickly and soon, a dozen locals in wellies were searching with torches, In the early hours of the morning, Angus McLean found her in his stable, snuggled in the hay.

'Just like the little Lord Jesus, Baloch,' she told him when he visited the hospital.

She was never the same after that night. A chest infection turned to pneumonia and she was left confused and incontinent. Life was so messed up. Nanna Rose had always been there for Hamish. She was a strong willed and stubborn woman, a fighter, but she couldn't fight this. She would have been affronted to be having toilet accidents at her age and to be fed like a bairn.

The endless questions were hard. When am I going home? What's your name again, lad? But in moments of clarity, what I am still doing here, Baloch? I'm past all this nonsense. 'Enough is enough,' she repeated.

He was heartbroken. Kind, loving, homely Nanna had been replaced with a sharp, distant, unrecognisable old woman. Nanna Rose was always up at six to watch the sunrise. This impostor had stopped getting out of bed

Hamish brought her a warm cup of tea with a straw and propped up her pillows, so she could drink and swallow comfortably.

'Enough is enough, Baloch, please.'

She placed her frail hand over his.

'ENOUGH!'

Hamish felt a chill go right through him. He had to help her. No-one deserved to suffer like this, a prisoner in her own body. Crushing the pills with the rolling pin and mixing them with the best sherry in her favourite mug, the one with the robin on. She always loved when the robin sat outside the croft window. He should have felt fear or guilt, but he had a sense of contentment, this was a gift to the woman who had given him so much.

He read aloud from his mum's Bible, as Nanna Rose offered him a thankful smile, slowly sipping her fond farewell

***

Hamish spent every waking hour pondering whether he had done the right thing. 'Thou shalt not murder', the Bible said. Was he going to go to hell? Was it really murder if she didn't want to be alive anymore? He was just helping his Nanna take her final steps, giving her a peaceful, dignified ending. No matter how much he tried to justify it, he carried the guilt on his shoulders. Unable to focus, his grades went down. He knew there would be a job for him on the farm regardless, but he couldn't bear to be part of their grief and feel that he was partly responsible. Instead of taking the school bus, he boarded the bus to Stornoway with his guitar and a school-bag full of clothes. His birthday money from Aunty Kathy paid for a ferry ticket and the bus from Ullapool to Inverness. Using the last of his coins, he asked the vending machine for a coke and a mars bar and found a quiet corner in the bus station. He wrapped himself up like a burrito in his orange sleeping bag. When he woke, his hands numb and his belly rumbling, he longed to be under his tartan duvet back home. His mouth watered thinking of hot toast covered in butter and strawberry jam, but this is how things had to be. He would find a way to start a new life. He had to!

After freshening up in the bathroom, Hamish made his way to Market Square, pausing outside the Victorian market to watch a busker play the saxophone. The mellow sound made him tingle inside and the clink of coins landing in his case was encouraging. In front of him, he could see the statue of a Highlander in his kilt. Hamish was intrigued by the sphinx which sat in the bottom. One hundred and forty-seven brave men had lost their lives in Egypt and Sudan. He wasn't brave. He was a coward, running away from his own family.

Singing outside Starbucks proved fruitful. There was a steady stream of students passing on their way to university and well-dressed professionals picking up their essential morning lattes. Without doubt, this was Hamish's favourite spot. His rugged looks and sense of humour meant he was really popular with the ladies. He had no interest in the bubbly blondes who would pose for a selfie with him. His attention had been captured by someone else.
Every morning, about half past eight, she would glide by with a smile. He was enchanted by the way her silk dresses clung to her curves and he often imagined how her hair would fall around her neck when she removed her hajib. One day, he might pluck up enough courage to buy her coffee.

Without warning, the sky darkened, and it began to rain heavily. Hamish ran for shelter in the building next door. The sign on St. Mary Magdalene's Church declared that all were welcome. He doubted that God would still welcome him. After all, wasn't murder the ultimate sin. He had never regretted it, but his secret was a huge burden to carry around.

It really was a beautiful building, lavishly decorated in red and gold. He shuffled on to the wooden pew and took a moment to admire the ornate ceiling, the columns and arches and the stained-glass window adorned with Jesus on the cross. He picked up the bible in front of him, something he hadn't done since the night he said goodbye to his nanna. He read the leaflet that lay inside,

'If we confess our sins, he is faithful and just and will forgive us.' 1st John, chapter 1, verse 9.

If only that was true, and God believed Hamish had done what was best. Instinctively, he closed his eyes and spoke to God silently.

'If you're listening, I do still believe in you, even if I don't understand why you can't fix all the shit in this world. Sorry God, are you even allowed to swear in a prayer? Anyway, I just wanted to talk about Nanna and everything. It was her choice, I was just helping someone I loved, right? I hope you let her into Heaven. She was pretty awesome and if she didn't deserve to get in, then who does? I don't care what happens to me, but I hope you can forgive me. While I've got your attention, there's this girl I like. and I was wondering if you could put a good word in for me. Thanks heaps. Well, Amen I guess.'

He felt incredibly guilty when he opened his eyes. It was meant to be a heartfelt apology, not a wish list. As he lit a candle a on the way out, he thought of his nanna. Her woolly cardigans and the smell of her home baking.

'Are you alright there, son? asked the minister.

Hamish nodded and made for the exit like a small boy in trouble

***

Every morning, Hamish's face would brighten, as he watched his beautiful, silk clad lady glide towards him. He loved the way her vibrant red and orange saris made her stand out from the crowd. She would give him a smile, while she dropped a treat in his hat. Amongst the coppers he found a kit kat, a Starbucks gift card and his favourite, a badge bearing a rainbow. The ultimate sign of hope. Maybe there was hope for a relationship with her. Maybe God was answering his prayer. Who was he kidding? Why would she choose him over a handsome, intelligent man from her fancy office?

He began to make a special effort in the morning. A spritz of Lynx, tying his dark curls into a neat ponytail and coupling his blue jeans with one of the Aran jumpers, Ruth had lent him. Her son was having a gap year travelling and had left his Winter clothes behind.

Hamish was on a mission. A simple smile turned into wishing her a good morning, chatting about the weather, and finding out her name- Pareesa. It was such a beautiful name. He practiced saying it out loud as he walked home. Home. His heart would always be back on the island, but Ruth had been so kind and generous, he really felt like he belonged in her cosy cottage.

Having spent the weekend plucking up the courage to ask Pareesa out, Hamish was dismayed to see her walking with a group of friends, not even looking his way. The following day, she handed him a hot chocolate and a warm chocolate croissant and stayed to chat while she drank her latte with a cinnamon bun. It wasn't quite the coffee date he had envisioned but it was amazing to hear Pareesa's melodic voice and learn more about her

'I'd really like to chat more,' he said, 'maybe we could go for a walk or something.'

'Sure,' she said, with a smile, 'I'd like that.'

After a few more coffees and walks watching the sun go down, Pareesa invited Hamish over for dinner. He was apprehensive as he rang the doorbell. She answered the door with a smile and placed a gentle kiss on his lips. As he passed the hallway mirror, he caught sight of his reflection. Pareesa was changing him, inside and out. She preferred him clean-shaven and he had to admit it looked good, but he would keep his long hair. That was not negotiable.

It had been a revelation to find that Pareesa didn't survive on curry and rice. He cursed himself for being so judgemental. Tonight, she had prepared a delicious meal, fillet steak with goat's cheese and peppers, crème brulee for dessert and a lovely bottle of red wine. Everything was so easy and relaxed when they were together. Hamish envisioned a great future for them. The only barrier was that she was there already, starting her career and owning her own place. He would be playing catch up. Pareesa was a little tipsy after the wine. There was a new sparkle in her captivating green eyes and a confidence that took him by surprise. Snuggled next to him, she let her delicate hand rest on his. It felt so right, as though they were meant to be together.

Pareesa brought out an advert she'd cut out of the paper. They were looking for an assistant teacher for a pop/rock course for teenagers. He was sceptical at first, but why not? The money was decent, and it sounded fun.

'I think it would be perfect for you,' she said. 'You'd be so good with the kids.'

'Thanks, that does sound great. I think I could make a difference, help them follow their dreams.'

Dreams...So many possibilities, opportunities. Lodging with Ruth and busking had been an adventure, but he wanted to be able to provide for Pareesa, like his dad had for his family. Pareesa wouldn't be a housewife though. She was a free spirit, full of ambition. Hamish felt sure this was only the introduction to a life full of adventures they would share together.

Skye

Everything we've done for you and this is how you repay us,' Esther yelled.

'Whatever, I never asked to live here anyway,' I mumbled.

'Watch your mouth, Lara! Now get out of my sight until your father comes home.'

I slammed the door and stormed upstairs to my room, threw myself down on my unmade bed and gazed at the roof. Bill wasn't my father, but he was alright. Not like Esther. She was looking for a pretty little girl with pigtails and pink dresses to take to ballet. Not me. Definitely not me! My name was Skye.

'What kind of name is that?' Esther had asked the social worker. That's when I became Lara.

I tried. I really did. To stick to their silly rules and curfews. If Mr Collins had kept his mouth shut, everything would have been fine.

Dear Mr and Mrs Baxter, we hope Lara is feeling better and are wondering if she would like some work to complete at home. Kind Regards, Gerard Collins, principal.

That's how they found out that I hadn't been to school for two weeks. It's pointless anyway. I'm crap at everything and they all think I'm weird.

'That's me in for the night', Bill announced as he locked the door. 'What a day, I'm just going to grab a beer and chill.'

'I don't think so. That little brat's been lying to us again. You'll never guess what she's done now,' she said, thrusting the letter at him.

Poor Bill. I often think he wants out of here as much as I do.

'Well, I'm sure there's a perfectly valid explanation. Maybe she's being bullied or something?'

'I doubt it. If there's any bullying going on, I'm sure she's the instigator. I don't know if I can do this anymore, Bill. You should hear the way she speaks to me.'

I giggled to myself. Bill was in charge of my allowance. He only saw the good Lara. The one who thanks Esther politely for tea and loads the dishwasher without complaining. I didn't know how he was going to react to this though.

'Lara, could you come down here please?'

Here we go. The interrogation begins...

'Sweetie, we need to talk about this letter. What's going on? Why haven't you been at school?'

'Where has she been? That's what I want to know' said Esther.

'Just give her a break. She has a right to explain herself'.'

'I just can't do it, Bill. The work's too hard and the teachers are always on my case.'

'Lara, you should have talked to us about this.'

'You're so busy. I didn't want to bother you.'

'Look, I'll see about getting you a tutor and I'll take you in tomorrow and have a word with Mr Collins.'

'Thanks Bill. I knew you'd understand,' I said, glaring at Esther.

Monday was an absolute nightmare. Mr Collins put me into remedial maths with the retards.

'Finally found some friends like you.'

Only Alexis would have the guts to speak to me like that. If I touched a hair on her head, her dad would have me locked up by the end of the day. I watched her walk away, swishing her hair with the rest of the blonde beauties in tow.

The moment I walked through the door; Esther was waiting for me.

'You might have Bill wrapped around your little finger, Missy, but I've had it with you.'

'Well you can't exactly put me back ten years later and ask for a refund!'

'No, but I can make life really difficult for you. For starters, you're grounded indefinitely, so you won't need your allowance and no internet or making calls.'

'Get real, Bill's never going to agree to that, you sadistic cow.'

She flipped and slapped me across the face. Awful as she was, she had never dared to hit me before.

I had to get out of there. I shoved some clothes in my school bag and next morning when Bill dropped me at school, I headed straight for Hutcheon Street, where Craig and his mates were squatting. Craig was the only person at school who really got me. His parents kicked him out when they found out he was gay. There was a whole crowd of interesting people and life was about having a good time. There seemed to be an endless supply of vodka and ciggies. Some guy asked if I wanted to try some acid. He handed me a blue square and I let it dissolve on my tongue, before taking a swig of coke to wash it down. It was pretty amazing stuff. Psychedelic colours whizzing around me. Even the stray kitten looked magical and rainbow coloured. I wanted to dance, and I couldn't stop laughing. I tried to chat to Craig, but he looked completely zoned out and my words weren't working properly. I felt like I was in some sort of alternative reality. The squat was a real hub of activity throughout the day and night. When I was high, life was awesome, but when it wore off, I was cold and low. There were always random strangers passing through and lots of money changing hands.

Until the raid. It was about five in the morning when they came. It all happened so quickly. Torches, sniffer dogs. Everyone who was sober just ran. I managed to get out through the broken window at the back and crouched down, hoping they wouldn't find me. I waited a couple of hours, just to be sure. My whole body shivering. My arm and leg bleeding from the broken glass. As I stood up, I was violently sick, and I suddenly realised how long it had been since I had a bath or shower.

I left and kept walking. I couldn't risk Bill and Esther catching up with me. That part of my life was well and truly over. Suddenly I felt an odd spinning sensation and I could feel myself falling. When I came around, there was a crowd staring at me. A friendly looking woman with a baby offered to call an ambulance, while a couple of pensioners crowded around to watch the show.

'No, I don't need an ambulance. I just skipped breakfast, that's all.'

'Well if you're sure. Go and get yourself a nice hot cup of tea.'

Seriously, like tea is the answer to all the world's problems. Did she have a clue how crap my life was?

'Here, drink this.' said a gentle male voice, handing me a bottle of water.

He was an odd-looking guy with his blonde hair tied in a ponytail, but he had kind eyes and a nice smile. He genuinely seemed like he really wanted to help.

'Can I get you a coffee? I'm Adam, by the way. You don't look too good.'

I didn't feel too good and a hot drink in a cosy cafe was just what I needed. I went straight to the bathroom and attempted to clean myself up a bit. Splashing cold water on my face felt amazing. When I got back, Adam had ordered me some toast.

'So how does a pretty girl like you get in a state like this?'

Without thinking, I just blurted out the whole story and he listened, like he'd known me for years.

'Would you like to come and stay with me and some friends for the night? Just until you get yourself sorted out. What's your name by the way?'

'It's Skye',' I smiled. 'Thanks, that sounds like a great plan.'

Adam drove into the country and up a long dirt track to their house. It looked like it was a working farm. There were some men working in the fields and an older woman hanging out washing. Inside smelled divine.

'We make all our bread from scratch'.' Adam explained. 'And we try to live off the land as much as possible.'

The house was huge. I wondered how many people lived here. Before the evening meal, Adam asked one of the children to say grace. A small boy in dungarees stood up and bowed his head.

'Father, thank you for our prophet Adam and for the wonderful food he has given us. Amen'

The food was delicious. Roast chicken and potatoes and apple crumble for dessert. There was a lovely warm atmosphere and they all seemed so happy. After supper, we gathered in the main room, where there was a log fire blazing. The older woman, Marion, sat at a harp and the woman with black hair grabbed a flute. Everyone started singing. I just listened. I didn't have a clue what the songs were, but the music gave me goose bumps.

As people started heading to bed, they told me how nice it was to meet me and gave me a hug. I couldn't remember the last time I had been hugged. It wasn't Esther's style. Adam put his arm around me reassuringly.

'So, Skye, what do you think of our little family?'

'Everyone's lovely and thanks for the meal. It was delicious. How many of the children are yours?'

'All of them' said Adam.

But there must be at least seven, I thought. Oh well, farmers have big families. Don't they?

'You can share with Louise and Katherine, upstairs, first room on the left.'

'Thanks heaps for helping me today.'

'You're very welcome, Skye, it was my pleasure.'

Next morning, I was treated to breakfast. Freshly squeezed orange juice, eggs, and more home baked bread. It was like a hotel. I thanked the ladies and asked where I could find Adam, so I could organise a lift to the bus station and leave this lousy town behind.

'He'll be out feeding the horses' said Louise.

I found him in the barn.

'Morning, Adam'

'Ah, good morning, Skye. I trust you slept well'

'Best sleep I've had in ages.'

'You sure looked like you needed it.'

'I was wondering when a good time would be to drop me off at the bus station.'

'You won't need to go to the bus station, Sweetie'

'Adam, you've been so kind. Thanks, but I really need to get far away from this town.'

'I don't think I made myself clear, Skye. You're mine now. You won't be going anywhere!'

He pushed me into the barn and kissed my neck. His breath was vile. I didn't have time to think. Adam pushed me forcibly down on the hay. I was paralysed with fear, trying to scream, but not able to make a sound.

'Wow, you haven't done that before, have you? 'Don't worry, Skye, God wanted me to be your first.'

Over the next few weeks, I learned how everything worked in the house. Adam could have any of the women when he pleased and with his consent, any of the other men could too. There were so many weird rituals. Under the full moon, we would make a circle and burn a foal or a lamb as a sacrifice, while Adam called out prayers and chants. If any of us dared disobey him, we would be punished. I didn't know exactly what this involved, but I didn't want to find out. I'd wanted so badly to escape from my life. From school and maths, Bill and Esther, but now I had become involved in something much worse. This kind of thing only happened in magazines.

When Adam said he was taking me in to town, it was a great surprise. He waited until it got dark and then we headed off. He explained that God was calling me to go 'flirty fishing.' My mission was to seduce someone and encourage them to come back to 'my place', where Adam would get them involved in our community

One of the perks of the house was that I could help myself to clothes, make-up, and perfume. I had made a real effort tonight and I was really happy with how I looked. I stood on the corner of the street and it wasn't long until a silver car slowed down and opened its window.

'Mr Collins!' This was God saving me.

Adam was charged with rape and holding me against my will and as for me, I'm back living with Bill and Esther and she can dress her granddaughter in as many pink dresses as she wants.

My little Molly. I don't care how she came into this world. I'm glad she's here.

Bennachie

My magical, mysterious mountain
I gaze in awe
At your silhouette on the sunrise

A celestial, celebration in the sky
Hues of yellow and orange bleeding together
A shimmering, spectacular sight

You call me to you and my quest begins
A tranquil walk through a tunnel of trees
The scent of pine, spruce and fir filling the air

In the silence, I can hear your song
The whispering wind, the babbling brook
The cuckoo's call

How many wonders does this forest hide?
Deer and red squirrels, running wild and free
A buzzard soaring above

The terrain changes before me
A colourful carpet of purple heather
Entwined with primroses and bluebells

The steep path climbs ever higher
Till with pride, I take the rocky steps
To the granite summit- the mither tap of Bennachie

---

[1] In the kitchen.

ACKNOWLEDGEMENT

Thank you to my wonderful family for their continued support and encouragement. Special thanks to my writing sisters- Jess, Wendy and Alison and fabulous tutor, Rosemary Dun, for making my writing journey such a positive experience.

2020- the year we were told to stay safe and stay at home, but not everyone is lucky enough to have this sanctuary.

Meet Edith, Finn, Hamish, and Skye and learn how their very different stories led them to a life on the streets.

Our granite guardian, memories of the promenade and Bennachie illustrate why Aberdeen is a great place to call home.

All proceeds from this anthology will be split between two charities to raise money to help the homelesss- Aberdeen Cyrenians and Crisis.

Printed in Great Britain
by Amazon